PRINCESS AND

FRIENDS

By Carol Anne Dunn

This book is dedicated to my grandnieces, Jessica and Paige, and my grandnephew Ethan.

Cover and Illustrations by Carolyn Frank

ISBN: 9781798513064

Printed in the United States of America
Amazon Publishing
Seattle, Washington, United States
https://kdp.amazon.com

Table of Contents

Chapter One

Hurricane

Princess's whiskers twitched. She had a strange feeling that things were about to happen. Her intuition was always right about these things. She continued watching her owners from the safety of under the bed; she could tell they were worried. She hunkered down and blinked her Sapphire eyes. Sadie, the cat next door, said she would be inclined to give up her "purr" for such eyes.

Thinking of Sadie, she remembered that she had not seen her for a day or two, perhaps she would know what a "hurricane" was and if it was dangerous for cats. She determined to ask her tonight if she saw her outside. Sadie was several years older and could be a very superior know-it-all at times, but Princess loved her friend's generosity of spirit and relied on her for companionship.

Princess and Friends

Sadie wasn't up to catching lizards these days but was knowledgeable. It was Sadie who had warned Princess against the "Skinks." These were the blue-tailed lizards that did a number on your head. Princess did not want to be considered a blue-tailed addict—catnip was bad enough. Princess loved catnip!

Princess quietly tip-toed into the bedroom and peeked around the door, which was slightly ajar, and from this vantage point, she could see the living room very clearly. Suddenly there was a flurry of activity from the porch. The sliders opened, and the outdoor furniture carried inside one piece at a time. There was some bad language. Princess was shocked when she heard this language being hurled about by her human owners. One human's toe was squashed.

She was beginning to become alarmed, especially when her litter box was lifted and carried inside. The bedroom sliders were boxed in with see-through shutters. The activity was entirely new, and Princess was beginning to become alarmed. The activity was mystifying. Well, that ruled out talking to Sadie. She would not be able to go outside now.

As the night wore on, the tension in the house began to rise. Eventually, her humans crashed into bed at one o'clock in the morning, and she was able to sneak up into the bed under the coverlet and curl up to a human body for warmth.

Since she had had her trip to the groomer last week, she had not been able to get warm. She had even "hissed" at Sam the groomer because Sam had left her in the dryer too long. A cat can only endure so much, and being clipped was terrible enough, but having to face the medicated bath once a month was almost unbearable. Princess had tried to explain on numerous occasions to her female human that cats don't like water, but somehow the message got lost in translation. Somehow her human was being very stubborn and ignoring the situation.

The next morning, Princess had another shock. Lured out from hiding by the promise of treats, Princess had been grabbed by her scruff, and given a pill and jammed into a new carrier. She sniffed with interest the fabric of the new carrier. Sniffing was difficult because there wasn't a lot of space inside to turn around.

Princess wondered if Sadie was undergoing similar treatment next door; however, all thoughts of Sadie fled from her head as she was picked up and unceremoniously dumped into the back seat of the car. Princess was about to protest, but her meow froze in her throat, for some reason she was feeling very peculiar and very sleepy—well, perhaps a quick nap would help her sort through things she reasoned. It was also time to take care of her fur—Princess was very particular about her grooming. Her friend Sadie was not quite as meticulous. But there again, Sadie was just a large tabby cat, she did not have Princess's beautiful cream coat and seal points. But Princess only completed half an ear, before she fell into a deep, dreamless sleep.

Princess awoke to find herself lifted from her carrier into something called a hotel room. She sat on the strange bed and surveyed this new environment. Princess took a few hesitant steps, and suddenly her back legs went out from under her. How very strange; she felt lightheaded and very, very thirsty. She espied her water dish and made it over to the counter, where she drank deeply from the cold refreshing water. Princess could not remember when the water had tasted so good; as a matter of fact, she could not remember being allowed on the counter.

Princess and Friends

During the following day, Princess became accustomed to the hotel room. Her humans spent a great deal of time glued to the talking box, but at least she was getting lots of strokes and lots of attention. Princess loved the attention.

On the second day, Princess sat on the windowsill and surveyed the dismal scene blow. The rain was lashing at the window with furious precision. Princess felt so glad she was warm and dry. Suddenly, her body froze, becoming rigid with concentration as she watched not just one but two pit bulls being led outside in the rain to do their business. So, they had dogs here. Princess always thought cats were superior to dogs, and now she had reliable confirmation— dogs were too stupid to use a litter box!

The next day her humans stopped for breakfast at something called the *River Rats*

Café. Princess, from a floor vantage point, glimpsed the river—a fast-moving river swollen with hurricane rain.

Princess sat impassively, blinking her beautiful eyes, watching the scene before her intently, missing nothing. Suddenly, a blue jay came hopping to the cage and peaked inside the carrier

"What kind of cat are you?" asked the Jay boldly.

Princess didn't usually talk to birds. However, since she was stuck here, it might be amusing to talk to him.

"I'm a Himalayan," she said courteously.

"Why is your face so black," asked the bird, "it looks like soot."

"It's part of my markings," explained Princess, that together with my tail, ears, and feet are my points."

"Points," said the Jay. "I have never heard of such a thing, how very strange."

Bertie, for that was the Blue Jay's name, looked curiously at the cage. "Why have they got you in a cage," asked Bertie.

Really, thought Princess to herself, *this bird is not too bright.*

"This is not a cage, but a carrier," explained Princess, "and it's the way I travel."

"You should grow wings," said Bertie, "much easier to get from place to place."

"Thank you," said Princess, "I will keep that in mind for future reference."

"You are welcome," said Bertie, and with that, he took off soaring into the air with agility and ease. *Show off,* thought Princess to herself as she watched Bertie disappear into the distance.

Later that night, as she sat on her back porch again, Princess related to Sadie all the high points of her trip. Sadie, her eyes glowing in the dark, listened to her neighbor's story with a thoughtful air. She gazed at Princess with an air of great wisdom.

"What you have experienced is called an adventure," she said.

"Oh, no," said Princess with confidence, "it was a hurricane, my humans said so, and they are never wrong!"

Chapter Two

Babies

Princess woke from a long, luxurious sleep to the sound of someone calling her name. Opening her beautiful sapphire eyes and looking up, she saw a small, colorful bird calling to her from the vantage of a nearby tree limb.

"Why Bertie," she said to the small Jay. "What are you doing here?"

"Hi, Princess," said Bertie, tipping his head to one side and regarding her with bright black eyes.

"I thought I would fly over and see how you are getting on after the hurricane. I am also house hunting."

"House hunting?" said Princess quizzically. "Are you looking to settle here?"

"Yes," said Bertie, looking slightly ill at ease and not his usual carefree, confident, and cocky self.

Princess and Friends

"I am thinking of settling down and starting a family."

"Why Bertie, that is wonderful," said Princess. She looked at the little bird and saw him ruffle his beautiful blue feathers. In the sunshine, they had a shimmering iridescence.

He is an excellent bird, thought Princess, *and despite his playful, cocky ways, he is a good friend*, she thought fondly. *He will make a terrific mate and will take care of his young chicks.*

"I am so glad you are here," she said. "Do you know what a baby is?"

The bird looked at Princess very seriously, "Princess, you are very naive sometimes."

"Well," said Princess politely, trying not to take offense, "I don't have your experience of the world, it is true. But I am trying to learn more. This is serious, Bertie. We have a baby coming to stay for three weeks in November, and I want to know what to expect."

"Babies," said Bertie, "are small humans and, unlike baby birds or kittens, they take forever to grow up. They are ugly things, since they have no fur, feathers, or hair, and they cry a lot."

Princess digested this information. The idea of a baby seemed worse than she had feared.

"And" said Bertie, ominously, "adult humans are enormously fond of babies. If you have a baby coming to stay, you had better be on your best behavior."

Princess thought this last piece of information was irrelevant since she always tried to be on her best behavior. However, she decided to overlook that remark since Bertie was fast becoming a good friend, and he certainly gave her another way of looking at the world.

"What I want to know," said Bertie, "is why you are caged? Your humans seem to keep you locked up."

"Oh, Bertie, this is my very own porch. I patrol it twice a day and make sure it is free from lizards and other pests."

"Oh," said Bertie, digesting this new information. "Well, I cannot think of anything I would like less than to be caged, but each to his own." With that, he took off, flying high into the air with a grace and ease of motion that was not lost on Princess.

I don't know which is worse, babies or Bertie, thought Princess crossly to herself. *That bird always has the last word.*

That night, sitting in the cool of the evening while listening to the frogs and buzz of insects in the night air, Princess decided to ask her friend Sadie, the cat next door, if she knew anything about

babies. Sadie, who was a tawny brown tabby with emerald eyes that glowed in the dark, looked at her small friend and took her time answering Princess's question.

"Babies require a lot of attention," said Sadie. "For the most part, humans do not like cats around babies. They are frightened that you might scratch the baby or play rough with the baby. Babies' eyes are not as good as cats' eyes. They do not focus as quickly as kittens' eyes do, and they are not as coordinated as kittens at the same age."

"You will have to be very well behaved around this baby and try not to interfere too much," added Sadie. "I know you are used to a lot of attention, Princess, but you must learn to share with the baby."

"Oh," said Princess, in a tiny voice. She was beginning to feel exceedingly small and insignificant, considering this new information.

The next day was Tuesday, and Princess was off to have her monthly trim at the groomers. She had formed a fast friendship there with a small puppy named Humphrey. He was a French bulldog with big, bulgy eyes and large bat-wing ears. Despite these comical features, he was a handsome individual and had a wonderfully lively spirit.

"Princess," yelled Humphrey excitedly as she came through the door in her cat carrier. "I am so glad you are here. Even if you are a cat, you're my age; all the other animals here are so old."

Princess grinned despite herself. "Humphrey, quiet, they will hear you." She looked at the little black Scottie dog that Sam was grooming on the table in the center of the room and saw that he had a tough time standing since he had arthritis in his back legs.

"Oh, Jock won't hear me," Humphrey grinned. "He is as deaf as a post."

Princess sat patiently in the cage next to Humphrey.

"Anything exciting been happening to you?" said Humphrey.

"Well," said Princess, "We are getting a visit from a baby in November. Do you know much about babies, Humphrey?"

"Oh, I know everything there is to know," said Humphrey, excitedly, itching an imaginary flea on his hindquarters. "We have two of them in our house!"

"Two," said Princess in wonder. "How can that be?"

"Oh," said Humphrey, "it is something to do with being a twin."

Princess stored this new bit of information. "Tell me about them and how you handle everything," said Princess.

"Babies are great fun," said Humphrey. "I play with them most of the day. They smell a lot, and you cannot understand everything they say, but they are great to roll around with on the floor, and they throw things at you." This information was a small revelation to Princess.

"Humphrey, you have cheered me up no end," said Princess. "I was beginning to think I was in for a tough time."

"Princess," said Humphrey, looking at her with affection. "You take life far too seriously. You must learn to chill out and relax. Remember, life is all a matter of perspective; it depends on which way you are looking at things, and what your point of view is at the time."

Princess thought this was sage advice. Humphrey showed some hidden qualities, and despite his comical appearance, he invariably made Princess see a different side to the box, as Sadie was wont to say.

Princess, Sadie would say, *all you have to do is picture the problem like a box and turn it around and see it from a different angle.* Sadie was usually right.

Eventually, November came and went, and Princess found out firsthand all about babies. Bertie was correct: babies don't have fur, feathers, or hair, and Sadie was right that babies do require lots of attention. However, Humphrey was bang on the money: babies are a lot of fun!

Chapter Three

Snake

Princess awoke one morning in early November and strolled out through the cat flap onto the porch to find Bertie waiting for her impatiently on a tree limb near the house.

"Bertie why are you here so early in the day?" said Princess, greeting the little Jay with warmth.

"Princess," said the little Jay, bobbing up and down with excitement. "I have found a home for Penny and me. It is a vacant nest, but I think it is well-built, and it is on the corner of the wetlands among the sandy oak scrub just behind your porch."

"Why, that is wonderful, Bertie," said Princess with a grin. "When will I be able to meet Penny?" She had never seen the bird looking so excited and enthusiastic.

"I am bringing her over this afternoon, and you will be able to meet her," said Bertie. He was hopping up and down and dancing on the branch.

"I have told her all about you, and she knows that you are a C-A-T! I had to explain that because birds and cats are not usually such good friends.

"Oh, I understand completely, Bertie," said Princess demurely. "Where is the nest? Can I see it from here?" Princess craned her head, trying to look through the scrub that bordered the other side of the creek.

"I am not sure," said Bertie diffidently. "Well, yes, maybe you can, if you climb to the top of your cat tree and look straight ahead." And, with that, he flapped his wings and soared off into the air.

"I will be back at one o'clock with Penny," he called back over his wings.

Princess looked at Bertie and realized with a start that he wasn't that good at flying, despite his showoff bravado. At their first meeting, Princess had thought Bertie flew effortlessly, but she now suspected that he kept close to home. He never seemed to drift too far from his territory. However, Bertie had met Penny, who lived in a neighboring region. The two young jays had decided to settle down in an area that he had inherited from his parents.

Princess ran to her climbing tree and leaped lightly to the top. She looked straight ahead, and there, through the branches of a live sand oak, she could just see a little nest hidden between the branches. She watched for the rest of the morning as the two little birds worked hard at repairing the nest.

She grinned to herself as she watched Bertie issuing instructions to Penny. He seemed to be responsible for the overall structural integrity of the nest, while Penny, who was a little smaller than

Bertie was crafting the inside with twigs and fiber from a nearby saw palmetto. *What industrious creatures the two little birds are,* Princess thought to herself.

Right at one o'clock, Bertie arrived with Penny, and the two birds took up residence on the nearby tree limb that seemed to be Bertie's favorite perch.

"Princess let me introduce you to Penny," said Bertie, his chest and head feathers fluffing up with pride. Penny, peeking her head around Bertie's, bobbed up and down as a way of greeting Princess.

"My," said Penny. "You are a beautiful cat. Bertie said that you were, and he was right."

Princess preened at this gratifying news. However, at that very moment, Mr. Dunn came out onto the porch, and he had a small flat dish of peanuts in his hand.

"I thought I heard you out here, Bertie," he said. "Oh, and you have brought someone to see us. See what I have brought you and your mate for a treat? Peanuts. I just knew it was a special occasion."

Mr. Dunn went outside the porch and placed a small saucer of peanuts under Bertie's tree and then went back into the house. Together, Bertie and Penny descended to the ground, and each picked a peanut. Then they flew to a branch and used their sharp beaks to break the peanut down.

"I cannot thank you enough," said Bertie to Princess. "Penny and I have been working hard all morning, and we are famished."

"I never knew you liked peanuts," said Princess. "However, I shall remember that they are a favorite."

Soon the little birds grew tired, and off they went to settle down in their new home. As the days passed, drifting into the hot, humid days of summer, they became a fixture in Princess's little circle of friends.

She loved watching them and noticed that many of the small birds would hide when Bertie signaled a call of alarm to Penny that there was a hawk or a snake in the vicinity. Pretty soon, she recognized his alarm call, and, without realizing it, she would be on alert for the birds.

One morning in spring, Bertie could be heard shrilling his alarm. By this time, Bertie and Penny had produced three small green eggs that had turned into three fluffy grey chicks. One particular gopher snake was particularly persistent. He had tried to reach the eggs many times.

On hearing Bertie's alarm call, Princess, who had perfect eyesight, rushed to her cat tree and was just in time to see the giant gopher snake eat one of the fledglings. What a horrible tragedy for the two young birds.

"Quick, Bertie," she loudly called. "You must defend your nest."

"Right on it, Princess," yelled Bertie as he dive-bombed the snake and pecked at its head. Penny, who was on the ground at the time searching for grubs, raced to follow Bertie in dive-bombing the snake.

The snake, whose name was Hercules, was quick to assess the danger to his head and slunk off down the tree. He came right by Princess's porch and was trying desperately to slide by unnoticed but was aware of a pair of blue eyes following him as he tried to pass by.

"What on earth were you thinking, Mr. Snake?" said Princess rather sternly. She was incensed to think he would steal from a nest.

Princess and Friends

Snake

"My name is Hercules," said the snake with a slight lisp. "A fellow has to eat once in a while."

"You may have to eat," said Princess, "but you don't have to eat my friends."

Hercules had the grace to look uncomfortable. He was quite an intimidating size, and his markings were attractive. He looked as if he were one long chain: his splotchy markings were most distinctive.

"Hercules, if I may call you by your first name," said Princess. Princess was loading on the charm, trying to appeal to the snake's better nature. "I am very fond of those two young birds, and I want you to promise me that you will leave them alone."

Hercules, who was a solitary creature and lived by himself in a burrow, was somewhat ashamed of his behavior—although, for a snake, it was perfectly natural behavior.

"I am sorry, said Hercules. "I promise to try and behave and hunt in other areas of my territory."

"Well, I guess that is something, at least," said Princess. She was still very cross with the snake, and, despite his size, she knew he was nonvenomous. "You really should be ashamed of your actions!"

Hercules mumbled something to himself and slithered away as silently and swiftly as only a snake can.

Bertie and Penny took some time to get over the death of their youngster. However, raising the two remaining chicks, a boy and a girl, took most of their attention. Princess quite often saw Bertie and Penny flying around collecting insects, acorns, weed seeds, berries, and anything else they could find. Princess even saw them caching acorns for the winter and burying them in the sandy ground under their tree. They frequently got into fights with Herbert, a local grey squirrel, who seemed to dominate any bird feeder in the vicinity together with a red-headed woodpecker named Jack.

Often, Princess would be trying to get some rest in the middle of the morning and could hear the jays and their noisy squabbles.

On these occasions, Princess would grin to herself: she thought fatherhood was suiting Bertie very well. He was asserting himself and employing his garrulous nature for the benefit of his family. She did not doubt that those two young jays would be an asset to any neighborhood.

Chapter Four
Christmas

It is Christmas, and Princess loves Christmas. Princess, the small Himalayan cat who lives in Florida, is lounging on her sheepskin pad on the sofa, watching the opening scene to Clint Eastwood's *Pale Rider*. However, the movie is not holding her interest, and although sleepy, she is in the half-hypnotic state that cats acquire when they are between sleep and waking.

Princess looks with sleepy interest around the rest of the house. The house looks particularly beautiful this year with the holiday decorations. The small tree sits on a small chest and glitters with ornaments collected by her family throughout the years. The lights are glittering red, orange, blue, green, and white.

The red and gold ornaments are glinting, shimmering, and twinkling on the tree in the half-light. Princess feels very serene and tranquil. Her family, Mr. and Mrs. Dunn, left the house earlier to go to the store to pick up a few things for Christmas dinner. In their haste to leave, the family had forgotten to turn off the TV.

However, Princess's attention is now focused on the tree and at the pile of parcels under the tree. She knows there is a small stocking for her buried under the mountain of presents.

Suddenly, Princess hears a noise from the dining room. It is a scratching noise as if someone were trying to lift a window. Princess's body becomes ridged. She is suddenly wide awake and on high alert. Princess's beautiful sapphire eyes grow huge as she sits up to listen.

Princess and Friends

There it is again, a distinct noise coming from the area of the dining room. Princess jumps effortlessly off the sofa and pads quietly to the dining room on the balls of her tiny chocolate feet. She doesn't believe her eyes -- there coming through the window is a small dirty leg attached to a foot encased in a tennis shoe that has seen better days.

Princess moves closer and tenses her body. Years of lizard hunting has conditioned her for the chase. She moves stealthy and quietly as she comes within a foot of the small leg.

Within seconds, she springs her attack and attaches herself to the leg, sinking her sharp, little teeth deep into the exposed flesh. A loud howl erupts from the other side of the window. Princess hangs on for all she is worth. The cries grow louder by the minute as the leg now tries to escape back through the window.

Christmas

Across the path is Frank and Orma's house. This house is where Sadie, Princess's best friend, a large tabby cat lives. Frank and Orma, Sadie's family and the elderly neighbors next door, hear the ear-splitting yells of the young boy as he tries to escape back through the window.

Frank and Orma rush into the yard where an incredible sight meets their eyes. A small, scruffy boy of about ten years old is trying desperately to escape the window next door with a little cat attached to his right leg.

Frank immediately sizes up the situation. "It's alright, Princess," he said softly, "you can release the boy now."

Princess reluctantly relaxes her grip, and Frank takes the small boy, who is balling his eyes out, next door together with Orma and Princess following behind.

Princess and Friends

Orma tries to look at the leg, which is bleeding quite profusely, but the boy keeps moving away from her. In the end, she gives him an old towel and tells him to wrap it around the wound. Frank asks the boy his name while Orma and Princess watch from the side-lines.

Sadie wanders up, "What's going on, Princess?" she asks with concern.

"I was just about to take a nap, and this young boy tried to break into the house," said Princess with certain amount indignation. "I didn't think too clearly, so I bit him."

"That was a rather drastic action," said Sadie. "What if you were hurt or even worse kicked?" Sadie looked at her friend in awe and thought to herself, *but it does show a certain amount of courage.*

Mathew, the young felon, looks at Frank, "It was wrong, but I just wanted a few presents for

Brook and Troy," he says hesitantly. Tears had made tiny rivers down his dirty face, and he looks pathetically at Frank as if willing him to understand.

"Who are Brook and Troy?" asks Frank sternly. "My brother and sister," said Mathew. "My mom's all on her own now that Dad has died, and she can't afford a lot this Christmas. I just wanted them to have a present each," he sobs, starting to whimper again. "Will I go to jail?" He looks fearfully at Frank.

Frank looks at the young offender and tries to maintain his dignity while suppressing a smile.

"That depends on..." he said, leaving the rest of the sentence hanging in mid-air. He has never seen a more pathetic or inept thief. Hearing a car pulling in next door, Frank rushes out to greet Mr. and Mrs. Dunn in the driveway with the story of the break-in and to bring them over to their house.

Mr. Dunn accesses the situation (he once worked at the Kennedy Space Center, where he was used to making decisions).

"That bite looks deep, Mathew, he says. I think I should take you to the hospital and then let your mother know that you are there."

Princess hearing Mr. Dunn make this statement knew that she would not be able to attend the hospital, but she did feel a little guilty upon learning that the bite was quite deep.

She tried to get close to Mathew and explain that she was only protecting the house, but Mathew did not seem inclined to be friendly. He looked fearful as she came near and started to whimper again.

Poor Mathew's mother, badly shaken by the arrival of Mr. Dunn at her door, drives with him to the hospital. At the hospital, Mathew receives a tetanus shot and two butterfly stitches to close his cat bite.

"I will not press charges, said Mr. Dunn. "Mathew was trying to do a good deed for his brother and sister, but just going about it the wrong way."

When Mr. Dunn arrived home later that evening, Princess learns that Mathew is doing fine and is back at home. Princess is still feeling "uncomfortable" at having bitten a human; however, she is somewhat mollified by a large bowel of sardines for supper. Mr. Dunn sitting in his large comfortable chair, strokes her after supper.

"You are a good, brave cat, and you protected the house, but try not to bite anyone next time," Mr. Dunn whispers in her ear.

Later that evening, as Princess sits contentedly looking up at the starry sky and listening for the eerie sounds of Florida night: frogs, birds, the hum of millions of insects, and -- what was that? -- Yes, Princess hears the chattering of a mother raccoon in the background.

Sadie, Frank and Orma's large, brown tabby cat, is amazed at Princess's courage. She had not seen the incident, but she had witnessed Princess's bite and had heard Frank and Orma discussing what had happened.

"Thank goodness you didn't get hurt, Princess," said Sadie with a gentle voice. "What were you thinking of attacking like that?"

"I don't know," said Princess with a yawn. "I don't think I was thinking of anything really... except to protect my house."

The next day the doorbell rings, and when Princess and Mr. Dunn answer the door, there is Mathew and his mother.

"Mathew has something to say to you, Mr. Dunn," said Sue, Mathew's mom.

The small boy, looking decidedly cleaner than the day before, looks up shyly at Mr. Dunn. "I'm so sorry to have broken into your house," said Mathew, "do you think Princess has forgiven me?"

"Sure, Mathew," said Mr. Dunn, smothering a grin, and Princess steps forward so Mathew can pet her, tail held high.

"I never thought a cat could attack as Princess did," said Mathew. The small boy, all shyness evaporating as he scratches Princess's ears, suddenly regains his enthusiasm.

"Can I please come and see her sometime? We live close by, just across the retention pond in the gray apartments."

"Tell you what Mathew," said Mr. Dunn kindly, "Why don't you come by next week on Wednesday if your mother lets you. I am going sailing with Princess." Princess's ears twitched at the word sailing. What was this sailing?

"Oh boy," said Mathew enthusiastically, "I would love that. Can I go, Mom, please?" Mathew's mother looks down at her young son.

"As long as you promise me you will help Mr. Dunn on the boat, and never, I repeat, never, break into anyone's house again."

"I promise," said Mathew solemnly.

"Mathew can swim well," said Mathew's mother, "And it would be good for him to learn something new."

Princess, sitting quietly on the mat at the front door, listens to the conversation and wonders about this "sailing." She will ask Sadie tonight what the word means. Princess thinks Mathew seems overly excited by the prospect of such an outing. Princess was not at all sure it was a good idea since this young man was the intruder who tried to break into her home. Well, she thinks to herself, only time will tell!

Chapter Five

Sailing Adventure

Princess, a small Himalayan cat who lives on the East Coast of Florida, was extremely excited. Today was the day she was going sailing with Mathew and Mr. Dunn. Mr. Dunn's first name was Chauncey, and he had asked Mathew to call him by this name. Chauncey had already fitted Princess out with a small, cat-friendly life jacket; he had also bought one for Mathew at the local Wal-Mart. Mathew was Princess's neighborhood friend, a ten-year-old boy with a friendly grin and freckles.

The doorbell rang, and Princess and Chauncey let Mathew into the house. He was excited and talked nonstop while they piled into the car the necessary things for their sailing trip—water, extra clothes, tea bags, cookies, and a few sandwiches.

Princess and Friends

The trio set off for Harborville over the old barge canal and parked. As Mr. Dunn and Mathew unloaded the car, Princess sat on the dock, feeling uncomfortable at the stares she received from passersby.

A cat on a leash was something that they had not seen in Harborville. A cat on a leash and life jacket was worth a second look. Why, some people even took a photo of her. Princess ignored the whispers and sat patiently on the grass verge, watching both the boy and the man as they loaded the boat, *The Stargazer.* Eventually, Mathew took the leash and urged Princess to jump onto the deck.

"Come on, Princess, you can do it," he said gently. Princess took a flying leap and landed lightly onto the boat.

"Princess let's look around," said Mathew as he stowed his possessions.

Sailing Adventure

The boat was a sailing boat with an inboard motor. It had a cabin and a compact kitchen and slept four people comfortably. While Mr. Dunn motored out of the harbor, Princess and Mathew sat up on the bow and watched the sides of the bank.

They saw a lot of exotic birds and a couple of alligators that were lounging on the bank, trying to warm up. Once on the river, Mr. Dunn called Mathew up to the bow of the boat and proceeded to give him lessons on how to get the sails up and steer the boat.

The boat suddenly lurched to the left, and at the same time, Princess saw something shimmering in the water. It was an enormous fish—no, it was two massive fish—no, it was a school of large fish playing in the water, jumping and arching their backs. They were playing with each other. Princess could see the fish were gray with a lighter underbelly.

Princess and Friends

Suddenly, Princess lost her footing and slid right into the water, letting out a massive yowl as she did so. As the cold water hit her, Princess let out another colossal howl. She was terrified and began fighting furiously to come to the surface of the water. Suddenly, a huge animal came up from underneath her and helped to bring her to the surface.

"Oh, thank you," she spluttered.

"You are welcome," said the animal with a funny chirping noise. "What kind of animal are you?"

"Oh, I am a cat," said Princess, catching her breath. "I belong to that boat over there. We were sailing, and suddenly I slipped off the bow of the boat. Fortunately, I have my life jacket on, and so I bobbed back to the surface with your help. Thank you so much."

"Just part of the service," said Sabrina, the dolphin. "It is not often we get animals like you in our part of the world."

"Do you swim?" she added.

"I don't know," said Princess. "I have never tried to swim before, but I am sure that I could learn if I tried."

"Well," said Sabrina, "all animals should swim if they are living in Florida."

"Ah, "said Princess, "that is extremely sound advice. How did you learn to swim?"

"I don't know," said Sabrina. "I grew up knowing how to swim. I think I was born swimming."

"Yes," said Princess thoughtfully. "I can see how that could be living where you live. You do swim beautifully."

Sabrina looked incredibly pleased with this flattery. Suddenly, Mr. Dunn was there with the boat and Mathew leaned down with the help of Mr. Dunn and picked Princess up out of the water.

"Thank you, Mr. Dolphin," said Mathew. "You rescued an excellent friend of mine."

Sabrina sat on her tail and waved to Mathew and Mr. Dunn, making squeaking noises as they sailed away.

"Wow," said Mathew. "That was a big fish. Thank goodness he rescued you, Princess."

Princess, her teeth chattering with cold, tried to tell Mathew that Sabrina was a "she-dolphin," not a "he," but her voice was waterlogged, and her fur matted from the water. She looked ten pounds thinner and very bedraggled. The water ran in rivulets off her coat and onto the deck of the boat. However, she soon got dry and was given a few treats to make her feel better.

That," said Mr. Dunn, "is not a fish; it is a mammal and is commonly called a bottlenose dolphin (*Tursiops truncates*). These mammals live in the sea along Florida's Atlantic and Gulf Coasts.

"Do you know, Mathew, that these mammals live to the age of thirty, and most are six to eight feet in length?"

Mathew digested this information and then asked, "Chauncey, what about the funny noise he was making?"

"These mammals use a system of echolocation, much like sonar, to determine their orientation," said Mr. Dunn. "They also make barks, clicks, and whistles to communicate with other dolphins." Mathew was impressed that Mr. Dunn knew so much about dolphins. Mathew thought he might write a paper on dolphins for his next science project.

"Those mammals are our State Saltwater Mammal; did you know that?" said Mr. Dunn. Mathew did not. He determined to do some research when he got home and could not wait to tell his mother what he had seen today. Mr. Dunn looked severe.

I should have tied both you and Princess down with tethers," he said. "Next time we go out, I will buy each of you a harness."

That night, while on the porch listening to the beautiful sound of night insects and the sleepy murmur of the birds as they settled down to rest, Princess told the story of the day's adventures to Sadie, the brown tabby cat next door.

"You do lead an adventurous life, Princess."

"Well," said Princess, "I am not sure that I would repeat this adventure. I was terrified for a while, but Sadie, I loved the fresh salt air and watching the water that seemed to change color as the sun shifted on the horizon.

We did see some fascinating birds." And, with that, Princess promptly fell asleep as she was—sitting up

Sadie looked fondly at her young friend. *She does lead a charmed life,* she thought to herself, as she curled up on her comforter and fell fast asleep.

Chapter Six

Skink

The team of contractors arrived early in the morning. Princess, who was having a catnap on the porch, was jerked awake by the noise of the four men moving heavy machinery around. Quickly forgetting the rude interruption, she watched with interest as the men set about their business.

From the vantage point of her climbing tree, she watched as the men sank four-inch metal pipes into the ground, using a hydraulic machine to drill the earth and eventually lift the whole porch pad by three and a half inches. Fascinating thought Princess to herself. Who would have thought that a solid block of concrete, with the right tools, could be adjusted as one solid piece?

Suddenly, Carlos, one of the workmen, gave a yell. "Oye, Miquel, look at this." Princess turned her attractive cream and chocolate head and looked where he was pointing.

"Why, it's a snake nest—a nest of baby snakes."

Carlos and Miquel quickly reached for a spade and scooped up the baby snakes. Princess watched as the tiny yellow and black wriggling things were shoveled and dropped into Snake Creek.

Bertie, a large blue jay with iridescent feathers, whom Princess had met during the hurricane, was also watching this operation.

"Princess, those snakes are not poisonous," he said.

"I know, Bertie," said Princess. "All the same, I am glad that Carlos and Miquel have removed them."

Skink

Bertie and Princess watched, from their respective perches, as the men put in angle irons underneath each corner of the porch and lifted it with a huge machine. Raising a porch was a big job and took almost the whole day.

As the men left, Carlos yelled out, "Buenos Noches, Princess." Princess particularly liked him. He was hard working and jovial. He sang as he worked, and she loved the sound of his rich baritone voice.

"Gracias, Carlos," said Princess. "Thank you for telling me about the Cuban sandwich." Earlier in the day, Princess had helped Carlos eat lunch.

"Did you know that the creation of Cuban sandwiches occurred in Tampa's Ybor City rather than Cuba?" Carlos had said.

"No," said Princess. "Why were they created, Carlos?

"Because the cigar workers needed a nutritious lunch," he explained.

"Oh," said Princess. "I must admit I love the combination of meats—the sliced roast pork and glazed ham, plus the Swiss cheese, but I am not too keen on the Cuban bread."

"Cuban bread is an acquired taste," said Carlos dismissively. "You, of course, have not lived there, so you were not brought up eating this fine bread, but my wife packs plenty of filling into the sandwich, so help yourself."

"And why a *Cuban sandwich* and not an *American sandwich*," mumbled Princess with her mouth full of delicious pork and ham.

"Ybor City was the only city in the southern United States populated and owned by immigrants. There were many different people there—Cubans, the Irish, Italians, and Germans— but it was the Cuban immigrants that settled Ybor and created the cigar trade. My great-grandfather was born there. It was a genuinely multiethnic, multiracial population," he said proudly.

"I can see why the Cuban sandwich was so good for the workers' lunches. It's full of protein," said the cat, happily accepting another tit-bit of cheese from Carlos. "I must admit, this cheese is delicious."

"I have plenty," said the workman. "Would you like to know the Spanish for a *cat*?"

"Si, senor," said Princess, practicing the few words Carlos had taught her at lunchtime.

"*El gato* is a male cat, and *la gata* is a female cat."

"Gracias, Carlos," said Princess, her blue eyes sparkling. She gazed at Carlos with her beautiful chocolate face and batted her lovely blue eyes.

"Saw that, saw that!" chirped Bertie, hopping up and down excitedly on his branch of a nearby live oak. "Princess, I do believe you are flirting with Carlos."

She chose to ignore the interested and (at times) intrusive Jay and contentedly purred as Carlos raised a hand to stroke her. *How strange different languages are,* thought Princess to herself, *and how smart of Carlos to be able to speak both English and Spanish.*

Princess was sorry to see Miquel and Carlos leave. Bertie was not. "They made too much noise," he said later that day.

"Bertie are you feeling okay?" said Princess kindly. "It's not like you to be so cross."

"I have a lot on my mind, Princess," said Bertie, and with that, he flapped his shiny blue feathers and soared off into the fast-approaching dusk. Although the porch was now firmly positioned, it still needed several new kick plates at the bottom and a new rescreen job. But although Mr. Dunn called many contractors the next day, they were too busy fixing porches damaged in the recent hurricane.

"We will have to wait, Princess," said Mr. Dunn. "I am relying on your hunting prowess to keep unwanted visitors off the porch. In other words, any stray lizards that lose their way will need chasing off."

So, Princess stepped up her patrols from twice a day to three times a day. She took her duties very seriously. Tippy-toeing on the pads of her feet, Princess patrolled like a Roman centurion guard, always vigilant.

The very next day, she caught a new variety of blue-tailed lizard. Indeed, she found it as tasty as Carlos's Cuban sandwich.

Princess and Friends

That night, Princess felt strange. She let out a strangled meow, which came out sounding like a very strange meow indeed—more like "Meooooww."

"I don't feel well at al-l-l-l," she wailed.

Mr. Dunn jumped out of bed. "Princess, whatever is wrong with you?" he said, concerned and bewildered.

She lurched into a wall, staggering to a stop. "Help!" she said feebly, "I don't feel well. I feel peculiar."

Mr. Dunn sprang into action. In his work at the space center, he was adept at dealing with emergencies before they became crises. Gently putting the cat into her carrier, he drove carefully but speedily to the emergency vet.

There, Dr. Williams, a young, newly qualified vet with large horn-rimmed glasses

that made him look knowledgeable and calm, examined her, looking specifically at her eyes.

"Has she been catching skinks?" he asked.

"Are they the blue-tailed lizards?"

"Yes," said young Dr. Williams. "There is no concrete proof one way or another, but certain cats that eat the lizards' tails will display these same symptoms. There is enough anecdotal evidence to strongly suggest that the symptoms Princess is presenting are linked with the blue-tailed skink. However, there is no scientific evidence to date. The skink has a wonderful evolutionary adaptation against predators. He loses his tail, and the predator is so astonished at the tail coming off, apparently wriggling of its own free will, that the skink often escapes."

"We believe that there is something in the tail, or it could be bacteria living on it, that somehow gets into the cat's system and deprives it of thiamine, and thus the cat acts like he has eaten poison."

"Good grief!" said Mr. Dunn in horror. "What is to be done? I cannot lose Princess. She is a valuable member of our family."

"Don't worry," said Dr. Williams.

"Fortunately, I have seen these cases before. We will keep her for a few days, put an IV in to stabilize her with fluids and medicine.

An IV means that she can receive her medication immediately."

Mr. Dunn breathed an audible sigh of relief, although he was somewhat perplexed at how they were going to get an IV into Princess's small veins. He questioned Dr. Williams about this problem.

Dr. Williams was very reassuring. "Mr. Dunn, we are used to dealing with very tiny and huge animals. We have all the necessary equipment to make Princess very comfortable as she undergoes her treatment."

Three days later, Princess returned home, much to the relief of all her friends. Even Bertie, who seldom displayed emotion, had tears in his eyes.

"Princess, it is so good to have you back to normal. "Sadie, the brown tabby from next door, looked at her friend lovingly. "Princess, things were too tranquil without you. When you're here, there is never a dull moment."

"Well," said Princess, "this is one adventure I don't think I'll be repeating anytime soon."

And the three friends laughed merrily, although underlying the laughter was more than a hint of gratitude and relief. They had their friend back once again.

Chapter Seven

Raccoon

Princess was on her favorite porch chair, enjoying the sunshine. A pool of sunlight highlighted her cream coat and dark chocolate face, paws, and ears. These chocolate parts were known as points, and she was immensely proud of her distinctive looks. She was sleeping peacefully, and every so often would give a little twitch as she dreamed of heaped plates of tuna and chasing lizards.

Suddenly, Princess's eyes popped open. A noise had disturbed her. She glanced upwards and hanging halfway from the top of the porch screened cage over a very spikey cactus was an extraordinary creature. It was not a cat (of that she was sure), and it was not a dog, but it did look like something in between a cat and a dog. The creature was bulky, and its hind legs were long. It had a grey-black coat and a white and black face with a sharp nose.

"Excuse me," said Princess rather crossly. "What are you doing, breaking into my porch?"

"Oh," said the intruder. "I did not know the porch was occupied. Does this porch belong to you?"

"Yes," said Princess firmly. "Your intrusive behavior has disturbed my rest." Princess was not feeling very friendly towards this strange individual. "What kind of animal are you?"

"Allow me to introduce myself," the masked bandit said. "My name is Rosa, and I am a raccoon."

"Oh," said Princess with surprise, her feelings of irritation evaporating at the chance to meet a raccoon at such close quarters. "I have heard of raccoons, but I have never met one before. Do you usually make a habit of breaking into porches?"

"Oh no," said Rosa. "However, you have sunflower seeds on your porch, and I thought they were going to waste, so I thought I would get some for my children."

By this time, Princess had recovered her usual good humor, and she looked at the strangely marked individual with interest.

"The sunflower seeds are for the birds," she said. "However, I am sure that we can spare some for your family."

Rosa needed no further encouragement. She hopped down with surprising agility onto the small summer kitchen counter that was to the side of the cactus and grabbed a handful of sunflower seeds, which she hastily crammed into her mouth.

Princess and Friends

Raccoon

"Rosa," said Princess thoughtfully. "Isn't that a Spanish name?"

"Yes," mumbled Rosa with a mouth full of sunflower seeds. "We have just moved here from Miami. My ancestors came from a small island in Mexico, where they still have raccoons. The island is called Cancun, and the raccoons there are not as big as the American variety."

Princess hardly heard what Rosa was saying because she was mesmerized by Rosa's paws, which looked for all the world like human hands.

"What are your children's names?" asked Princess, liking her new friend's face now that she could see it closely.

"I have twins," said Rosa proudly. "Their names are Ricardo, Jr., and Isabella. They live with me in a den in a tree located in the wetlands behind your house."

"How exciting," said Princess. "I would so love to meet them."

"Well," said Rosa happily, "I am sure that I can arrange that; however, I must go," she said. "We raccoons are primarily nocturnal, you know."

"That is interesting," said Princess. "What does this word 'nocturnal,' mean?"

"It means," said Rosa, jumping with lightning speed from the porch counter to the cactus on up and out of the hole she had previously cut into the mosquito netting on the roof of the porch, "that we are mainly active at night."

Mr. Dunn is not going to be too pleased with that hole, thought Princess to herself, and she was right. Later that day, Mr. Dunn discovered the breach in the screen of the porch. He was none too happy as he looked upward and saw the big, gaping hole and the ragged edge of the mosquito netting. Mr. Dunn grumbled to himself as he went back into the house and called a screener, who came out later that afternoon and repaired the hole. He also put the sunflower seeds in a sealed box-like container and put the box into a cupboard on the porch.

Later that night, Princess was sitting listening to the evening sounds on the porch with her friend Sadie, the brown tabby cat next door, when they were startled to hear a chittering noise coming from the trees. Appearing out of the dusk was Rosa, and behind her were two tiny baby raccoons.

"These are my kits," said Rosa, beaming with pride. The kits sat chittering together on the tree right in front of Princess's and Sadie's porches. "Oh," said Sadie. "They are so darling. How old are they, Rosa?"

Rosa was startled by Sadie's voice. She had not spotted the sizeable brown tabby sitting on the porch next door, but she could see the emerald eyes glowing in the dark. However, despite being startled, Rosa could not help showing off her two young kits to the two cats.

"They are three months old," said Rosa.

"Sorry, Rosa," said Princess. "This is Sadie, my best friend. She lives next door to me, and we have become excellent friends.

Rosa looked sternly at her two offspring. "Say hello, Isabella and Ricardo, Jr."

The two youngsters chorused their "hellos" and looked bashfully at the two cats.

"We loved the sunflower seeds," said Isabella. "Thank you so much." She was the braver of the two young kits.

"Well," said Rosa, "we must get along. I am teaching them how to forage for food."

"Bye," chorused the youngsters, as they disappeared into the Florida night.

Two days later, Princess was again sleeping in the sun on her porch when she was suddenly jolted from sleep by a pitiful screaming sound. She raced to the porch screen and saw that the gardener had put out a cat trap for feral cats just behind Sadie's house, and there, huddled to one side of the cage looking pitiful and shivering with fright, was Ricardo, Jr. He was mewing, whining, and crying all at once.

"Hold on, Ricardo, Jr.," said Princess soothingly. "I will fetch Mr. Dunn, and he will soon have you out of there."

Princess raced into the house. She raced up to Mr. Dunn, who was sitting peacefully in his chair, reading a magazine.

"Meow, Meow," Princess cried, jumping on his lap and sitting squarely on the magazine. Poor Mr. Dunn had no other option but to listen to Princess.

"Whatever is the matter, Princess?" said Mr. Dunn. "This is not your normal behavior. I had better see what is going on outside that has upset you. You are usually such a level-headed little cat; something must have troubled you."

Princess raced up to the screen, stood on her hind legs, and meowed to show Mr. Dunn the cat trap with the little raccoon inside.

"Oh, dear," said Mr. Dunn, sizing up the situation immediately. "This is too bad for the little fellow. Don't worry, Princess. We will have the little raccoon out of there in no time," he said, as he opened the screen porch door and raced outside.

Mr. Dunn undid the cat trap door and tipped the cage carefully so that little Ricardo, Jr., could escape. Ricardo, Jr., ran into the dense Florida bush without a backward glance.

Later that same evening, Rosa emerged out of the dense bush.

"Princess," she called in a whispering voice. "Are you there?"

Princess and Friends

Princess emerged from her cat flap set into the sliding glass door.

"Rosa," said Princess joyfully. "I am so glad to see you. How is little Ricardo, Jr.?"

"He is fine, Princess, thanks to you. He is staying home tonight, resting after his scare. He will know in future to stay away from such cages."

"Don't be too hard on him, Rosa," said Princess. "He is very young, and they bait the traps with cat food, so, in a sense, he was trying to forage."

"I know," said Rosa. "But if you had not heard him, and he had stayed in the trap for any length of time, he could have died. It doesn't bear thinking about," said Rosa with a shudder. She closed her eyes as if to block out some horrible picture that only she could see.

Princess smiled at Rosa. "Rosa," she said soothingly. "Nothing bad happened, and Ricardo, Jr. has learned a valuable lesson. Don't torture yourself."

"Princess," said Rosa. "Being a parent is painful at times. I thank you from the bottom of my heart for helping little Ricardo, Jr. If ever you need help, you can call on me."

And, with that, she disappeared once more into the night, leaving Princess alone to stare at the moon that was just beginning to emerge and light up the night sky with a strange, watery, silver light.

Chapter Eight

Phoebe

Phoebe was a small cat who lived in Pelican, the village next to Cormorant Village, the community where Princess and her humans lived. Every morning, Mr. and Mrs. Dunn would walk around both villages to keep fit and trim. Some mornings, it was an effort for the Dunns to wake up, but usually, Princess helped them by jumping on the bed and pouncing on their bodies, which were hidden by the bedclothes, making it a game, so that eventually, one or the other would get up and feed her. Princess would not give up her jumping routine until someone got up to feed her.

Phoebe

One hot July morning, Mr. and Mrs. Dunn met a small, fragile-looking cat whose name was Phoebe. She belonged to a house nearby. Phoebe was a very independent cat.

Born on a farm in Sarasota, Phoebe did not like living in a home. She only ever went in when she wanted to eat. This fact distressed her owner because, in Florida, there are many hazards that cats could encounter, such as alligators, lynx, and wild coyotes. Phoebe had her left ear clipped. A clipped left ear indicated she had been picked up by a "Trap-Neuter-Return" team.

Phoebe must have been homeless in a cat colony somewhere, but she still retained her good looks. Her coat was several shades of beautiful apricot, black-brown, and a tiny touch of white. However, she did not have a tail. Instead, she had a small powder puff, rather like a rabbit's tail.

Phoebe's tail would fluff out when she was happy or afraid.

"Well, hello, Phoebe," said Mr. Dunn. "It's sweltering today, so I would get under the shade in your yard if I were you."

"Meow," said Phoebe, understanding Mr. Dunn immediately and heading for a bush on her property so that she could lie in the shade and stretch out. At that precise moment, her owner, Grace Webb, a rather large woman with a round face, came out looking somewhat flustered and distressed.

"Mr. Dunn, I have to ask you whether you could feed Phoebe while I am away visiting my sister, who is very sick."

"Certainly. How often do you feed Phoebe?"

"I leave her dry food out all the time, but I put fresh water out for her every day, and I also leave some water for her outside the door. If it rains or thunders, she goes into her little cabin by the front door."

"Do you think she would live on my back porch?" said Mr. Dunn. He did not like the thought of Phoebe alone in a thunderstorm. Thunderstorms in Florida could be quite frightening at times.

"I don't know," said Mrs. Webb, dubiously. "She might."

"Let me take her home with me and see if she will settle in with Princess. If she stays on my porch, it would be much better for her, and I will keep you posted on her progress daily by telephone."

Mr. Dunn came back later that day with a cat carrier and took Phoebe with him together with her water bowls, her cabin, and her feeding dish and supplies. Phoebe was a little apprehensive when he put her into her carrier, but Mrs. Webb spoke soothingly to her and assured her she would be fine.

Mr. Dunn was not so sure. Phoebe was a very independent cat and was used to living outside, but Mr. Dunn was determined to try.

Princess, on the other hand, knew something was up at home—her litter box arrived in the kitchen, and her outside door was closed.

Later that day, Mr. Dunn arrived with a cat carrier. Princess caught a glimpse and was horrified! *They were getting another cat—were they not happy with her?*

"Come on, Princess, this new arrival is only for a week or two," said Mr. Dunn. He rubbed her cheeks and face with an old towel and took another old rag to rub Phoebe's face and cheeks. Then he introduced the other cat's towel to each cat. Princess sniffed Phoebe's cloth, and Phoebe sniffed Princess's towel.

Both cats were well adjusted, as Princess had lots of friends, and Phoebe had lived in a commune, so it was only a matter of days before both cats were cohabiting on the porch.

One day, later that same month, Princess asked, "Why is your ear snipped?"

"Well," said Phoebe, hesitantly, "because I was picked up by the Trap-Neuter-Return (TNR) for feral cats' program."

Princess digested this information. "What kind of program is that?"

"The program is located in most Florida counties," said Phoebe, warming to her story.

"The tip of a cat's ear is snipped to identify that the cat as neutered or spayed. Spayed means that I can no longer have kittens." Princess remained silent, digesting this information.

Finally, she asked hesitantly, "Does this hurt you?"

"Oh no," said Phoebe with a grin. She realized, by looking at Princess, that Princess had never imagined such a situation in her young life.

"The cat is neutered under an anesthetic so that the cat does not feel anything. While sleeping, the cat's ear is snipped to let future trappers know that the cat is part of the TNR program. Cats may also receive injections to protect them from certain diseases."

"Why were you living in a colony, and what does feral mean?"

Phoebe considered Princess's question and tried to think of the best way to explain.

"I was wild as a kitten," she said. "Wild and lawless. I ran away. The comforts of the farm where I grew up did not appeal to me. I wanted adventure and excitement, so I joined a community of like-minded cats who were living on the street. I guess you could say that I wanted the freedom to do my own thing."

"Weren't you frightened of ending up in a pound or being hurt?" asked Princess.

"Oh, no," said Phoebe. "I loved the freedom it gave me. I would roam the port and look for fish, sit on the sidewalk and look at the traffic, or travel with my compatriots, who were also feral. Feral means wild," said Phoebe.

"I would hunt and catch my food, and I was young and fit. I thought I was invincible. In our commune, we shared everything—food and responsibilities. For a while there, it was a great life."

"However," Phoebe continued, "I reached adulthood. As time went on, a cat who was nothing short of a bully appeared within our group. I could not take his bullying, so I left in search of a new adventure. Eventually, by hitching a ride on a truck, I ended up here."

"How did you get your name?" asked Princess. "It is most unusual—although, I must admit, it suits you somehow."

"Ah," said Phoebe. "It is an ancient Greek name. The farmer who owned the barn where I was born was a retired Lutheran preacher, and he said it was Greek for bright. When I was born, my apricot fur was so bright it made me different among all the other kittens. He said I was a bright glowing spark among all the black and grey tabbies. Phoebe was a Titan and associated with the moon--and no, Princess, I am not exactly sure what a Titan is or was, so you will have to ask someone else."

Phoebe

Princess grinned at her new friend. "You are so exciting, Phoebe, I'm happy you came to stay for a while. I do hope you will be here for my birthday next week—so many of my friends will be here. We will be eating tuna fish cakes as a special treat."

"That sounds exciting!" she said. "I'm sure that I will still be here because I overheard Mr. Dunn on the phone, and Mrs. Webb's sister is still in the hospital." And with that, both cats curled up on their sheepskin mats and fell fast asleep.

Princess dreamt of communes and the freedom to travel and Phoebe of having a cozy home and plenty of food. True, she had made her life sound exciting, but she had not told Princess of the many times she had gone hungry and thirsty. There was a lot to be said for living in a comfortable home.

Bertie, the blue Jay, was sitting outside the porch cage and had been listening to the cats' conversation. Camouflaged by leaves, the cats had not seen him.

Bertie was deep in thought. He thought that Princess was too naive and gullible at times. Bertie hoped that she wouldn't get it into her head to try the nomadic and wild existence of a cat commune.

Ferals were dangerous felines, and he did not want her influenced by their wild and lawless behavior. Bertie considered Princess a friend, and Bertie would always look out for her. Phoebe was all right as cats went, but he knew that she was not telling the whole truth about life in a commune.

Chapter Nine

Boots

Princess was forlornly sitting in a cage at Sam, the groomer. "I am here far too early," she muttered to herself. She tried to settle down on the small carpet that was in her cage. The rug was Berber: durable, itchy material, and none too comfortable. She was just trying to soften it a little by kneading it with her claws when the door opened, and in came Humphrey, a French bulldog.

"Humphrey," she called, "how are you doing? I am so glad to see you. I thought I was going to be stuck here by myself."

Humphrey grinned happily. "It is so good to see you, Princess. How are all your friends back in your village? Have you had many more adventures?"

"Things are pretty quiet right now. But I have made a delightful new friend named Rosa. She is a raccoon and the mother of twins, just like your family. If I had not met you, I would not know the meaning of the word *twins*."

Humphrey looked at Princess and then at the cage opposite and saw that they were not alone.

"Princess, you aren't by yourself here. Look at that small cat in the cage across from you."

Princess looked and looked, but all she could see was a black pillow. "You imagine things, Humphrey. There is only a pillow."

"Princess, my eyesight is good, and I am telling you that is a small cat."

Princess looked once more, and sure enough, the small pillow began to move.

Boots

"Well, I never!" said Princess. "You may be right."

Humphrey and Princess began to call out to their neighbor, and slowly, the bundle started to unravel itself, and a small cat emerged. The newcomer was black with four white paws and an entrancing white smudge on her nose, and her eyes (Princess was always looking at cats' eye color since she regarded her eyes her best feature) were like topaz. *Those eyes are arresting,* thought Princess to herself.

"What is your name?" Princess and Humphrey called out, almost in unison.

"My name is Boots," said the small cat. "I am depressed and do not want to talk to you." She turned her back on them and hunkered down, facing the wall. This behavior troubled the two friends. Humphrey decided to try again to engage the young cat in conversation.

Boots

"Now, Boots," said Humphrey gently, "no trouble cannot be helped by discussing it with friends. I know that we have only just met, but it might help if you talked to us about what is troubling you. We have a wealth of experience between us, and we might be able to help you."

Princess was impressed by her young friend's gentle voice and maturity. Slowly, Boots began to unbundle herself again and faced the two animals across the way, dejectedly hanging her small head.

"You cannot help me. No one can," Boots said sadly. "You see, I used to belong to a nursing home in the center of town. I received room and board, and I had a very responsible job of visiting everyone that was bedridden and trying to cheer them up. I would stay a few hours and purr and purr so that everyone knew that they were loved and appreciated." Boots looked down at the floor, and slowly two tears began to roll down her face.

They hit the grating of the cage where they bounced off and landed on the tiles below.

"What happened?" said Princess sympathetically, by now completely engrossed in the story.

"The nursing home was bought out by a huge corporation, and the new manager said that she could not have cats running around the place. It was unhygienic, and the patients were at risk, she said."

"Imagine that," said Princess hotly. "Why, everyone knows that pets are good for the health of humans. I heard that on the news," she said, smugly turning to Humphrey, who seemed to know quite a bit more about the world than she did.

Humphrey, his tongue dangling from his mouth (he looked like he was grinning even when he was not), was distractedly scratching an imagined flea. "Now, Princess," he said, "let Boots continue her story."

"There is not a lot more to tell," said Boots. "They had to find a home for me pretty fast, especially after my years of service, but to find a home on such short notice was very difficult, so finally, Dr. Peterson, one of the vets here, said that she would take me and try and find me a home. However, I have been here for over two months."

"That is the most outrageous story I have ever heard," said Princess with a certain amount of emotion. "Why, Humphrey and I can find you a home. No one should have to endure what you have had to."

Boots still hung her head and looked at her front paws. "I don't want to be a burden to anyone," she said.

Humphrey looked at the little cat, and his whole body trembled with excitement. "You are no burden. Princess is right: we have lots of contacts. We are bound to find someone in need of a little cat for companionship. Just leave it to us." Humphrey was always game, whatever was needed. Some people might call him impetuous, but Princess loved his enthusiasm.

Later that day, when Mr. Dunn came to pick up Princess, she drew his attention to the noticeboard by sitting on his foot and meowing. He saw the flyers about Boots. "We will take some of these and post them in the neighborhood," he said, giving Princess a loving pat on the head. Humphrey's family also took some of the flyers.

Later that day, Bertie dropped by for a visit, and Princess told Bertie the whole story of Boots' predicament. Bertie was knowledgeable jay, and he covered a lot of ground when he was flying around, so she felt sure that he would spread the word. She also told Rosa and Sadie.

However, it was Sadie who found a home for Boots. The lady next door to her had moved away, and new owners had moved in. She heard the new lady telling Sadie's human, Orma, that she was looking for a friendly cat to keep her company. She did not want a young kitten to train but would love to have a young cat that was house-trained and used to people.

Orma called Mr. Dunn because she had seen in the village newsletter that Boots needed a home. The very next day, Mr. and Mrs. Williams drove to Dr. Peterson and looked at Boots. It was love at first sight.

Later that night, as all three cats were taking in the Florida evening air, Boots introduced herself to Sadie and thanked Princess.

Princess and Friends

"It is so good to meet you, Boots," said Sadie. "One can never have too many friends."

"That is so true," said Princess. "How are you settling in, Boots?"

Boots' whole demeanor was different now that she had new humans to look after, thought Princess to herself why she looked like a different cat!

"I love it here," said Boots happily. "My new owners have never had a cat before, so I am training them in all our cat ways, and they are learning so quickly. I love tuna, and they are feeding me tuna twice a day, and they have bought me some nice toys. I have my bed to sleep in and this lovely sun porch to take a cat nap should I need it. Life could not be better!"

"We are indeed lucky cats," said Sadie, "to live near each other and have loving humans. It's as well to remember with gratitude just what a comfortable life we cats have in this community."

And with that, all three cats dozed off still sitting upright because they had all had a long and tiring day.

Chapter Ten

Birthday Party

On the dawn of Princess's birthday, Princess and Phoebe were curled up on the porch asleep. They did not see the early sunrise that filled the porch with a golden light, bathing the two cats with a glow making their fur coats seem alive with fire. Phoebe's fur was stunning, including the apricot patches, which seemed to take on a life all on its own.

Sadie, the brown tabby next door, was awake as was Boots, the little black cat who lived next door to Sadie. They were whispering together, excited by the thought of the day's upcoming events. The two friends were eager for the day to begin. They were excited about the party and finally meeting all Princess's other invited friends. They also joined

Birthday Party

together and bought Princess, a new travel carrier with airy mesh panels and a sheepskin cushion.

Rosa, the raccoon, hiding in the trees just outside the porch, was chattering excitedly to her mate, Ricardo Sr., and the twins. It was their first party, and the youngsters were beside themselves with excitement—they could hardly speak. Bertie, his wife, and two young sons were invited. Bertie was up early and swept the nest out before his wife and children were awake. He took off flying to visit Mathew in the grey apartments. He knocked on the window with his beak. "Mathew, time to get going." chirruped Bertie. "You are helping Mr. and Mrs. Dunn with the party today."

Mathew raised his head from underneath the pillow and opened one bleary eye. He saw Bertie and got up and raised the window. "Thanks for waking me up, Bertie," responded Mathew as he gently caressed the top of the bird's head. "I will be there just as soon as I have my breakfast."

At nine o'clock, Mathew arrived to help Mr. Dunn pressure wash the porch. Princess and Phoebe made themselves scarce by disappearing into the house as they heard the water hitting the tiles as it cleaned the porch. Phoebe and Princess sat at the kitchen bar and watched Mrs. Dunn as she made tuna fish patties. Mathew soon joined her.

"Just wash your hands, Mathew, and you can help shape the patties."

"Wow, Mrs. Dunn, this smell is delicious."

The two cats sitting quietly on the bar stools suddenly "meowed," in agreement. Their mouths were salivating at the prospect of tasting such fantastic food. Phoebe had never smelled anything so good.

"Yes," responded Mrs. Dunn. "I left out the squirt of Crystal Hot, or you can use tabasco." "I know the cats do not like anything too hot, although I am sure Ricardo would love them with the tabasco."

"What are the ingredients?" asked Mathew.

"Cans of tuna, Dijon mustard, white breadcrumbs, lemon zest, lemon juice, chopped fresh parsley, chopped fresh chives, green onion or shallots (I used fresh chives), fresh pepper, one raw egg, olive oil, and butter to sauté in the skillet," replied Mrs. Dunn. "There now," she continued as she added the last ingredient—the raw egg, "that's about right. You mix this up and form the patties, Mathew. Divide the mixture into equal parts and form into a ball...that's right. Now flatten into a patty. Place the patties on this cooking tray lined with wax paper, and we will chill them for an hour."

Princess and Friends

While the patties were chilling, the doorbell rang. Phoebe and Princess went to answer it. There was an official-looking man with a large box.

"I am looking for Princess Dunn," said the delivery man as he looked at his roster.

"That's me," meowed Princess.

"Here you go, young lady," said the delivery man. "I am going to give this box to this nice young man behind you. I think this is a little heavy for you."

Mathew carried the box to the counter and opened it to show the cats. Princess and Phoebe climbed up on the counter stools and looked. Inside the box was a giant cake shaped like a fish. It had brightly colored scales. Next to it, in a small plastic bag, were three even brighter colored candles.

"Oh my," exclaimed Mathew enthusiastically. "Take a look at this, Mrs. Dunn."

Birthday Party

Later that day, at four o'clock, the guest began to arrive. Mathew was the door greeter. The first to enter was Humphrey and his human, Sally. Humphrey greeted Mathew and then rushed out on to the porch, which was a festival of color with brightly swaying balloons, Chinese lanterns, and streamers. The long table situated in the middle of the room was festive with a green tablecloth, recyclable paper plates, and bowls of water.

"Princess," yelled Humphrey, "It's so good to see you."

"You, too," said Princess, introducing Humphrey to Phoebe. Humphrey sat down at the table. Soon the seats were full of friends and families. Boots and Sadie arrived with Orma and Frank. Rosa and her family came via the porch door together with Bertie and his family. Boots noticed that instead of drinking from their bowls, the Racoons washed the lovely hot tuna fish cakes in

their water bowls. She thought that this was strange and oddly repetitive behavior.

After the tuna patties (they were a sensational hit with everyone), Mathew brought the cake out with the three candles. Everyone gasped at the cake shaped like a tuna and colored an azure blue and orange. The cake was a splendid creation—the fins and tail were outlined in orange icing, so they contrasted nicely with the rest of the fish. Everyone sang "Happy Birthday" to the best of their ability. Some were louder than others. Humphrey stole the show by throwing back his head and howling at the top of his lungs. His enthusiasm was contagious, although several of the smaller guests jumped at the noise.

Next, the extraordinary little gang of friends all feasted on vanilla ice cream and cake. By this time, the light was failing on the porch, and the Chinese lanterns lit up the dusky sky with a magic glow. What a wonderful time the friends were having together, chattering, and finding out about each other and their life stories. As the light began to fade, the little raccoons and Bertie's two youngsters began to look very sleepy. They departed, and slowly everyone else followed. There was one friend who missed the party—Sabrina, the dolphin.

Princess and Friends

She was away traveling in the Bahamas, visiting distant relatives. Princess, who understood the meaning of family and friends, had a strange hunch that she would see Sabrina on her next sailing trip.

AUTHOR

Carol Dunn started her story-telling career by telling ghost stories to her two young sisters while hiding under the bedclothes late at night. She later went on to work for NASA as a marketing writer.

Princess and Friends

She lives with her husband and one small cat in Florida. Her cat Princess inspires her writing.

ACKNOWLEDGEMENTS

Most of the research for this book was accomplished via the Internet. Florida State has a wonderful website that lists all the state animals that are Florida State Symbols. The Florida State Saltwater Mammal is the Porpoise or Dolphin.

The Florida Scrub Jay should be the State Bird since it is the only endemic bird to Florida. I wanted to draw attention to the Florida scrub-jay because the species is threatened, due to man's environmental encroachment and the fact that the bird has adapted itself to only one type of habitat.

For information on the Scrub Jay, I researched The Cornell Lab "All about Birds," Wikipedia, Audubon Field Guide, and the Florida Fish and Wildlife Conservation Commission. I also accessed livesicence.com to learn about the behavioral habits of gopher snakes.

Princess and Friends

All these sites deserve a big "thank you" for providing easily accessible and understandable information. These sites offer invaluable information for children and adults alike.

Made in the USA
Monee, IL
14 February 2021